The
Bermuda Triangle
Incident

THE UNEXPLAINED

The Bermuda Triangle Incident

Terrance Dicks

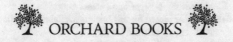 ORCHARD BOOKS

ORCHARD BOOKS
96 Leonard Street, London EC2A 4RH
Orchard Books Australia
14 Mars Road, Lane Cove, NSW 2066
ISBN 1 86039 630 5 (paperback)
First published in Great Britain by Piccadilly Press Ltd 1997
First paperback publication 1998
Text © Terrance Dicks 1997
The right of Terrance Dicks to be identified as the author of this
work has been asserted by him in accordance with the
Copyright, Designs and Patents Act, 1988.
A CIP catalogue record for this book is available from the
British Library.
Printed in Great Britain

Chapter One

VANISHED

'Calling tower. This is an emergency.' The pilot's voice was tense. 'We seem to be off course. We cannot see land.'

The speaker was Lieutenant Taylor, in command of Flight 19, a routine training mission. It was December 5th, 1945 and World War Two had been over for several months. That morning, five US Navy Avenger bombers had taken off from their base in Fort Lauderdale, Florida. Their mission was to carry out bombing runs on some wrecks on a sand bank just off the island of Bimini near Bermuda.

The mission had been completed and the planes were now returning to base.

At least, they should have been.

The message came again.

'We cannot see land. Repeat, we cannot see land.'

The controller was surprised by Lieutenant Taylor's message. It was a straightforward flight, weather conditions were reasonable, and Taylor was an experienced pilot.

'What is your position?'

'We are not sure of our exact position. We cannot be sure just where we are. We seem to be lost.'

The controller told Taylor to fly due west. The little squadron had to be *somewhere* off the Florida coast, and this course would bring them in sight of land.

Lieutenant Taylor's reply was distorted by static.

'We don't know which way is west. Everything is wrong – strange. We cannot be sure of any direction. Even the ocean doesn't look the way it should.'

Taylor said he thought he was somewhere off the Florida Keys – an incredible distance away from his correct flight path.

Suddenly Lieutenant Taylor announced that he was handing over command of the squadron to Captain Stivers, his superior officer, who was piloting one of the planes.

Stivers seemed just as confused as Taylor.

'We are not sure where we are,' he reported. 'We think we must be 225 miles south-east of base. We must have passed over Florida and be over the Gulf of Mexico.'

More static and then Stivers' voice came again.

'It looks like we're entering white water...'

Another voice broke through the static.

'We're completely lost...'

Those were the last words ever heard from Flight 19.

A rescue plane was despatched, a huge Mariner flying boat. It had a thirteen-man crew trained in rescue operations, was equipped with every kind of rescue equipment, and carried enough fuel to stay in the air for 24 hours.

It was never seen again.

The giant flying boat simply vanished – as completely and mysteriously as the missing flight of Avengers.

A fleet of ships and aircraft set off to look for

the missing planes. 18 ships, 242 planes, and an aircraft carrier with 34 more planes took part in the search.

They found nothing, not even wreckage.

The missing Avengers were found 45 years later, on the bottom of the ocean ten miles off the Florida coast.

No trace of the missing flying boat was ever found.

I closed the book – a rather lurid looking paperback called *True Horror Stories* – and sat back thoughtfully.

The vanishing of Flight 19 is one of the most famous mysteries connected with the Bermuda Triangle, but it's by no means the only one. Ships have been vanishing there since the time of Columbus. Now I was trying to find out why...

My name's Matt Stirling, and my father, Professor James Stirling, works for the Department of Paranormal Studies in an American Research Institute. As a matter of fact, Dad pretty well *is* the Department. I'm his unofficial assistant.

My parents split up soon after I was born, and naturally I stayed with Mum. Years later she was killed in a motoring accident and I went to live with an aunt and uncle. Just before my fifteenth birthday, they retired and went to live abroad.

Suddenly Dad found himself stuck with a son he'd never really met, and I had an unknown father on my hands.

Not surprisingly, it turned out to be an edgy relationship.

Dad's an eccentric genius, arrogant, intolerant, bad-tempered and bloody-minded.

As for me – well, I'm quiet enough on the surface, and I can manage to control my temper – usually. Friends and teachers have been known to tell me I'm as obstinate as an entire team of mules.

Dad and I are too much alike to enjoy a peaceful relationship. But we're fond of each other underneath it all, and we get on surprisingly well – with the occasional stormy patch.

Dad's a scientist with a string of degrees, specialising in space research. When the space race died down and research funds dried up, he was more or less shanghaied into the Paranormal Studies job. As far as he's concerned, he's marking time until a proper scientific job turns up. Meanwhile, a lavish salary and unlimited expenses help him to be miserable in comfort.

Dad's a born sceptic as far as the paranormal is concerned, which isn't a bad attitude for an investigator.

Personally, I try to keep an open mind...

Just recently, some very strange experiences investigating UFO sightings in Australia opened it even further.

Dad and his job were the reasons I was reading up on the Bermuda Triangle.

After our strange experiences in Australia we were looking around for another project. I'd suggested the Bermuda Triangle and Dad had agreed. I'd been researching the subject through books and the Internet, and I told Dad that if we were going to get any further it was time for a field trip.

He'd got up early that morning to go to a breakfast meeting in the West End with Dr

Byrnes, one of the American directors of the Institute, who just happened to be in London.

I wandered around our top floor flat in Hampstead, watching the rain lash down against the windows and wondering what to do with myself. In theory I ought to have been doing some studying – Dad's educating me at home, a job he takes very seriously – but I didn't really feel like it.

Telling myself I'd start work in a few minutes I switched on the television and got hit by one of those weird coincidences that happen more often than you might think.

The TV was tuned to one of those round-the-clock rolling news services, and as it came on a serious-looking announcer was saying, ' – still no trace of the plane which disappeared recently over the Bermuda Triangle. The aircraft, which was carrying several international VIPs, left a military airfield in Fort Lauderdale three days ago, en route for an unnamed destination in the Bermudas. Shortly after take-off, the pilot reported abnormal weather conditions. Soon afterwards all communication with the plane was lost and it failed to reach its destination.

'A rescue operation was mounted and is still in progress but so far no trace of the missing aircraft has been found.'

A map came up on the monitor screen behind the announcer, and he went on to fill in some background.

'The term Bermuda Triangle is usually taken to cover the area of sea encompassed by a line from Florida to Bermuda, from Bermuda to Puerto Rico, and from Puerto Rico back across the Bahamas to Florida. Sometimes it's called the Devil's Triangle. Over the years hundreds of ships and planes have vanished there without trace, with the loss of thousands of lives...'

He began going over the best-known Bermuda Triangle stories, including the one I'd just been reading about, the vanishing of Flight 19. I knew most of the stories already, and after a while I switched off.

I was still brooding over the weirdness of the coincidence when the telephone rang. It was Dad.

'Matthew? Pack!' he said with all his usual warmth and charm. 'We leave in an hour.'

Then he slammed down the phone.

I went to my room and packed my big holdall. I'd assembled a fair library of books on the paranormal and related subjects by now and there were several books completely devoted to the Triangle. I packed them to study further when I had time.

If we were off to investigate the Triangle that meant Bermuda or possibly Florida, which would be a long flight. I like working on planes. Nobody distracts you, there's nowhere to go, and they bring round food and drink at regular intervals.

Some time later I heard footsteps on the stairs. The flat door burst open and a wet and irritable Dad burst in.

He threw his raincoat on a chair.

'Have you packed?'

I pointed to the big holdall in the little hall.

'Just finished.'

'What about my suitcase?'

'You'll find it on top of your wardrobe.'

'You haven't packed for me?'

'You want a Jeeves, hire one. The Institute will pay.'

Dad was outraged.

'But the car's coming in fifteen minutes!'

'You'd better get a move on then.'

We glared at each other for a moment, then Dad stormed into his bedroom, grabbed the suitcase, opened it, flung open drawers and started chucking things in more or less at random.

Dad's been a scientific big-shot for so long that he's used to devoted assistants dancing round him, eager to fulfil his every whim. When we first started sharing the flat I had to take a firm line to convince him things weren't going to be the same at home. Otherwise he'd have had me cleaning his shoes and polishing the silver.

I followed him into the bedroom and began sorting things out, removing his winter underwear and Russian fur hat from the suitcase. I didn't mind helping a bit, once the principle was established.

'Where are we going?'

'Miami, initially.'

'Tickets?'

'At the airport.'

'Did you know there's been another disappearance in the Devil's Triangle?'

I told him about the missing plane.

Dad sniffed dismissively. 'There's no reason to suggest anything other than natural causes. It's an area of extreme weather conditions. There are deceptive calms followed by sudden storms.' His voice took on his lecturing tone. 'There are also certain electromagnetic anomalies that might well confuse an aircraft's navigational instruments. Did you know – '

'That it's one of only two places on the earth where the compass needle points to true north not magnetic north?'

Dad blinked.

'Yes, as a matter of fact I did,' I said airily, blessing my *True Horror* paperback. 'It confuses the fish, you know. Sometimes they swim upside down.'

Dad grunted and went on with his packing.

Very soon we were in the limousine speeding

towards Heathrow.

'Why all the rush?' I asked. 'What happened at the meeting?'

Dad frowned. 'I'm not sure. It was all rather odd. I told Dr Byrnes about our Bermuda Triangle project, and suggested a field trip...'

'And?'

'He seemed willing enough. He said he'd suggest it to the Institute and let me know their reaction. Then he got an urgent transatlantic phone call.'

'Who from?'

'I've no idea, he went off to take it in his room. Ten minutes later he came back full of apologies, said the Bermuda Triangle project was now top priority, and would I please leave for Miami on the next plane. All travel arrangements would be made, and I'd be briefed on the situation – whatever that means – on arrival.'

I thought for a moment. 'Bet you it's got something to do with that missing plane I told you about.'

'Oh I doubt it,' said Dad. 'What could one more missing plane have to do with us?'

I didn't bother arguing with him. 'Is that all?'

'Pretty much. Oh, he made a bit of a fuss at first about you coming too. He seemed to think there might be some element of danger. But I told him that if you didn't go I didn't go either, so that settled that.'

I was silent for a moment.

It had been partly obstinacy, of course. Dad can't stand anyone telling him what he can or can't do.

All the same, it was decent of the old boy to stick up for me.

'Thanks,' I said at last.

Dad grunted, a sure sign he was embarrassed.

'Not at all. You do have your uses, Matthew – even if you're not a Jeeves!'

I always think that the longest part of any journey by air is the business of actually getting on to the plane. All the same, our departure from Heathrow went amazingly smoothly. We were definitely being treated as VIPs.

It made a nice change from our Australian mission, when the authorities had spent most of their time telling us to clear off. Our first-class tickets were waiting at the airline desk, together with a top-class groveller of a company representative. We were whisked through security and passport control into a luxurious VIP lounge, where a handful of expensive-looking people were hanging about, enjoying the free drinks.

One of them, a tall, thin, crew-cut young man in horn-rimmed glasses, seemed to be taking an excessive interest in us, although he looked away hurriedly when I met his eye.

We were ushered from the lounge onto the plane and the flight got under way. Dad got stuck into the free champagne and I unpacked some books from my hand luggage and began revising my Bermuda Triangle research.

The Triangle certainly had a pretty sinister record. Its victims included a fleet of Spanish treasure ships in 1502, an American sailing ship in 1843 and a British frigate in 1880.

Even the coming of steam made little difference. A cargo vessel vanished in 1918, and in 1921 *ten* ships disappeared.

In 1925 a Japanese freighter got into trouble and sent out one last mysterious message.

'Danger like dagger now. Come quick.'

The ship, like so many others, was never seen again.

The disappearances continued during and after World War Two – including the famous Flight 19 affair.

Since then the disappearances have continued, sometimes at the rate of one a month, right up to the present day.

You might have thought planes would be safer than ships, but it didn't seem to be the case. A giant US Superfortress was lost, a British airliner vanished with all its passengers...

There was more – much more. It wasn't exactly ideal reading for a long plane journey.

The flight went on – and on and on and on. I read, listened to the audio channel, half-watched a couple of movies.

Every now and again unbearably bright and cheerful air stewardesses came round with food and drink.

Dad borrowed one of my Bermuda Triangle books and flicked through it before he fell asleep.

When I strolled down the aisle to get to the toilet, I saw that the tall, thin type with the crew-cut was with us on the plane. He was still making a production out of not looking at me.

I lay back in my comfortable seat, half-dozing, Bermuda Triangle stories drifting through my mind. One in particular...

An arriving passenger plane sent a message to Miami Airport Control. 'We are approaching the field. All is well.'

Then – you've guessed it – the plane vanished. It never reached Miami. In fact, it was never seen again.

All in all I was quite relieved when the long flight came to an end at last, and the Captain's relaxed Southern drawl announced that we were about to land at Miami Airport. For all I knew, we might have ended up in the twilight zone.

Miami Airport was vast, ultra-modern and confusing, but fortunately there was another company representative waiting for us when we got off the plane. We were hurried through security and immigration and into a waiting limousine.

Somewhere during the process I caught sight of the tall young man from the VIP lounge. Interestingly enough, the businessman look was gone and he was wearing jeans, sunglasses and a Hawaiian shirt. But it was him all right, still over-interested in us, and still trying unsuccessfully to hide it.

Miami itself was a sprawling city of tall white buildings, wide freeways and palm trees, all bathed in bright sunshine. It was incredibly hot, but the limousine was air-conditioned. It took us directly to an anonymous-looking office block in downtown Miami.

A lift took us up to a luxurious little conference room, where we were introduced to a serious looking, balding, middle-aged man in rimless glasses. His name was Simmonds and he told us he was 'with the Agency'. Exactly what Agency we never found out.

He offered us coffee and made a solemn little speech thanking us for our cooperation.

Dad waved it aside. He was in a grumpy mood, probably due to too much in-flight champagne.

'What cooperation?' he asked. 'All I know is that we've been rushed out here with indecent haste. It would be a great help if you could tell us what we're supposed to be helping you *with!*'

Before Simmonds could answer, I said, 'If all this has got something to do with security, maybe I should tell you that we were followed here from London. Tall, thin character with crew-cut fair hair. He was at Heathrow, he was with us on the plane, and he was at the airport here in Miami. I think he followed us here – there was a Cadillac convertible hanging on behind us on the freeway.'

Simmonds chuckled, and touched an intercom on the desk.

'Better get in here, Chuck, the kid

blew your cover.'

The tall young man came in, still in his tourist disguise.

'This is Chuck Roberts,' said Simmonds. 'He's with us. I had him keep an eye on you on the way over – just to make sure nobody else was keeping an eye on you.'

Chuck gave us an embarrassed nod and sat down.

'Now we've got the cloak-and-dagger games over,' said Dad acidly, 'perhaps we could get on with the briefing?'

'Three days ago,' said Simmonds, 'a small military transport plane set off from Fort Lauderdale heading for one of the smaller islands in the Bahamas. It was carrying three senior representatives from the Intelligence communities of England, France and America, on their way to a top level security conference.'

I gave Dad a triumphant look, which he loftily ignored.

'It was on the News back in England,' I said. 'They didn't mention the Intelligence side of things though.'

'We're keeping that under wraps,' said Simmonds. 'As you know, somewhere over the Bermuda Triangle the plane disappeared.'

'Just like Flight 19,' I said. 'And they didn't find Flight 19 for 45 years ...'

Chapter Two

RESCUE MISSION

Mr Simmonds blinked behind the rimless glasses.

'We were rather hoping for more rapid results than that!'

'How much more rapid?' asked Dad.

'We've got three days.'

Apparently the three bigwigs had been bound for a sort of pre-conference conference. In three days' time, Intelligence chiefs from all over the world would be arriving for the main event. And if the missing three weren't there...

'We'd be at a massive disadvantage from the very beginning,' explained Simmonds. 'Not only that, if word of the disappearance gets out, people will start wondering who was responsible. It'll create an atmosphere of suspicion that could wreck the entire conference.' He sighed wearily. 'We can't admit that they're missing, can't afford to be seen looking for them. The Intelligence community is a very small world.'

'But you are looking for them?' snapped Dad. 'I presume you're not leaving it all to us?'

'Sure, we've got teams out. But they've got to be discreet. It kinda slows things down.'

'So where do we come in?' I asked.

Simmonds looked embarrassed.

'Well, I guess it's pretty much of a long shot. We're just covering all our options. You see, there are already all kinds of weirdos poking around here.' He caught the look in Dad's eye and cleared his throat. 'No disrespect, Professor. There are guys hunting for sunken treasure, investigating the Bermuda Triangle... A couple more won't cause much comment. There's just a chance you might pick up something everyone else missed.'

'I see,' said Dad grimly.

'And the great thing is this,' said Simmonds eagerly. 'Your cover story is absolutely genuine. Anyone checks up, they'll discover you really are Professor James Stirling, the famous spook hunter!'

Dad drew a deep breath and I cut in before he blew up.

'What exactly do you want us to do?'

'Just see if you can find out anything about what happened to that plane, and where the three missing people might be if they survived. We'll be grateful for any hint, any clue...'

Simmonds hesitated. 'To be honest, Professor, there's another reason for asking you to become involved.'

'And what might that be?' asked Dad suspiciously.

'We have to cover the possibility, however unlikely, of – of alien involvement,' said Simmonds. 'You and your son, Professor, are amongst the very few people who know the truth about our contacts with aliens.'

'Do we?' I asked. 'Know the truth, I mean? Nobody in Australia seemed to want to tell us anything.'

'You know most of the little there is to know,' said Simmonds. 'You can forget all this conspiracy nonsense, all this baloney about captured alien spaceships and captive alien astronauts. Our contacts so far have been extremely limited and fairly disastrous.'

'There's the matter of Operation Thunderball, Chief,' began Chuck. 'Shouldn't we cover – '

'That's classified, Chuck,' said Simmonds firmly. 'No need to get into that.' Chuck subsided, and Simmonds turned back to us. 'As far as alien encounters are concerned – you seem to have done a lot better than most of us during that business in Australia.'

I remembered a limp alien figure on a stretcher, and a green four fingered hand reaching out to me. I didn't say anything.

'On the other hand, maybe there's no alien involvement at all,' Simmonds went on. 'Maybe it was just a natural disaster.'

'I get the feeling you're not telling us everything,' said Dad. 'It's hardly fair to expect us to work in the dark.'

'Believe me, Professor, I'm telling you all I can. This whole project is classified – top secret, need-to-know-only, the lot.'

'It's asking a great deal all the same.'

'Ah, come on now, Professor,' said

Simmonds. 'At worst it's a free holiday in Florida and a chance to investigate something in your field. All expenses paid, mind you. Go where you like, hire what equipment you need, everything's on the Agency.'

Dad turned to me. 'What do you say, Matthew?'

I considered for a moment, pleased that he'd consulted me.

'To be honest, I don't think there's very much chance of our being useful. But I suppose we ought to do what we can.' I looked at Simmonds. 'Is there anything more you *can* tell us? Anything at all?'

'All we've got is the time of the last message from the plane, and an estimate of its position – if it was still on course when it disappeared.'

Dad frowned. 'Is there any reason to think that it wasn't?'

Simmonds shuffled some papers on his desk.

'The last message is kinda peculiar. The pilot said everything seemed strange, nothing looked right, not even the sea. He said he was completely lost – not far from the Florida coast!'

The words sounded chillingly familiar. I thought of the last words of Flight 19.

'Did he say anything else?' I asked.

Simmonds studied the report. 'This last bit is really weird. Someone shouted, "What's that? It looks like a giant dagger – " then transmission broke off.'

I remembered the last words of the doomed Japanese freighter.

'Danger like dagger...'

' "All kinds of weirdos poking around," ' said Dad broodingly.

I grinned. 'I thought you'd like that. Don't forget you're now a "famous spook hunter"!'

'To add insult to injury, they don't really want me at all. They want you, just in case your alien friends crop up!'

We were driving north from Miami along Interstate 95, heading for Fort Lauderdale. By now we'd swapped the airport limousine for a rented Cadillac convertible, driven by Chuck Roberts, who was to look after us during our stay.

'Chuck's kinda new to the Agency,' Mr Simmonds had explained. 'Less chance of him being recognised.'

Considering that we were both complete amateurs at this espionage business, assigning us a trainee agent seemed to make it a clear case of the blind leading the blind, but who was I to argue?

Chuck drove us on into Fort Lauderdale, a seaside town close to Miami. Divided by miles of man-made canals, it's been called the Venice of America, which is stretching it a bit.

It looked a pleasant enough place though, bathed in the eternal Florida sunshine. Lots of posh waterside houses, each with a big boat moored on the doorstep.

Chuck drove us to a downtown hotel on Los Olas Boulevard where we all checked in. Then he disappeared, promising to come back first thing next day.

I checked out my room, played around with the 50-channel TV set for a while and went next door to see Dad.

He was stretched out in an armchair by the

window, speed-reading the Bermuda Triangle book I'd loaned him on the plane.

He tossed the book aside as I came in.

'All this just confirms my original opinion,' he said aggressively. 'Ninety-nine per cent of these stories can be accounted for by natural causes: stormy seas, sudden winds springing up. Add the possibility of freak local magnetic forces confusing navigational instruments...'

'Quite right,' I said cheerfully.

'You agree with me?'

Dad seemed disappointed that I wasn't giving him an argument.

'Certainly I agree with you. Ninety-nine per cent of UFO sightings are just lights in the sky, ninety-nine per cent of ghosts are the wind, or stray cats knocking over dustbin lids. It's that odd one per cent that concerns us.'

Since he couldn't disagree with that, Dad shifted his ground.

'This entire mission is a nonsense. I don't see what we can possibly do. I don't know why we're here and I don't know where to start.'

'We can do the obvious,' I said.

'Which is?'

'Get Chuck to hire a boat and we'll visit the area where the plane disappeared.'

'You seem to have everything worked out, Matthew,' said Dad grumpily.

Suddenly he grinned. 'I said you had your uses. All right, since I haven't any better ideas – any ideas at all, come to that – we'll follow your plan!'

Chuck turned up next morning, all bright-eyed and bushy-tailed, eager to know what he could do for us.

'We need a boat,' said Dad. 'A vessel big enough to take us out to the area where the plane disappeared. Something safe, seaworthy and reasonably comfortable.'

'We'll need a good crew as well,' I said. 'Dad's no sailor and neither am I.'

'No problem,' said Chuck immediately. 'The Agency charters a special boat down at Bahia Mar for this kind of operation. The captain's a guy called Clancy.'

According to Chuck, Bahia Mar was the biggest marina in Florida. I could well believe it. It was a whole city of boats, moored in neat rows to a maze of pontoons and walkways. Some of the boats were enormous luxury yachts, the kind that have a ballroom and a swimming pool on board. You could plug in to the marina's utilities, sit in the saloon drinking cocktails and watching TV and never think about going to sea at all.

There was every other kind of craft imaginable. Sleek ocean-going yachts, modest cabin cruisers, everything from a mini-liner to a rowing boat.

Chuck led us to a quieter, more workmanlike part of the marina and up to a shabby, sturdy-looking tub with a wheelhouse and a sizable cabin. Her salt-stained paint was an inconspicuous grey, and she was called *'Betsey'*.

'She doesn't look much, but that's deliberate,' said Chuck. 'Underneath she's state-of-the art, twin diesels, latest navigational equipment, the lot.'

We went on board and were met by a laconic nautical type in the standard jeans, T-shirt and yachting-cap. Captain Clancy had faded blue eyes, a brown leathery face and a stubby grey moustache.

There were a couple of crewmen as well, both younger versions of Clancy. I never got to know their names.

In the wheelhouse Clancy produced a map and Dad gave him the coordinates we'd got from Simmonds – the estimated position of the VIP plane when it vanished.

'We'd like to go out to that area and cruise around as long as possible,' said Dad.

Clancy nodded. 'Sure, no problem. We've got auxiliary fuel-tanks. I'll need some time to take on fuel and supplies. Once that's done we can stay out for days if you like.'

'What about our cover story?' asked Chuck. 'What do we pretend we're all doing out there – if anyone asks?'

Captain Clancy thought for a moment. 'Lots of little islands around, you can land and explore. Most of 'em are supposed to have pirate gold buried somewhere. Anyone sees us, you can pretend to be treasure hunters. We've got metal detectors and all kinds of other gear on board.'

'Is there really treasure out there?' I asked.

Clancy grinned. 'So folks believe. I've done quite a bit of treasure-hunting myself, between jobs for the Agency. Never found much though. If you get tired of looking for Spanish gold you can do some scuba-diving, or fishing...'

He paused for a moment. 'None of my business, but you know the missing plane area's already been thoroughly searched? They covered it when the plane first disappeared, sent a whole fleet of boats and search-planes. Didn't find a thing, no wreckage, nothing.'

'Never hurts to look again,' said Dad.

Clancy shrugged. 'Suit yourselves... Well, give me an hour to take on fuel and supplies and we'll be ready to cast-off.'

Chuck said he'd stay on board to help Clancy with the preparations, and Dad and I went off for a look around. By the time we'd looked at a few hundred boats we felt we'd seen enough.

Eventually we found a waterfront café called 'Rico's', a scruffy little place, crowded with tough-looking waterfront types. The villainous-looking character acting as the waiter had a drooping moustache, an unshaven chin and burning black eyes. He looked as if he'd cut your throat for ten cents and get rid of the body for another dollar. Still, there didn't seem to be anywhere else. We went inside, Dad ordered a beer and I asked for a Coke, and the waiter waved us over to a table.

Dad was hot and tired by now and in a grumpy mood.

'I can hardly believe we came all the way over from England on this wild goose chase,' he grumbled, as the barman brought our drinks. 'And with only those coordinates to go on...'

I did my best to cheer him up. 'Never mind. If we find the San Domingo treasure we'll go back home millionaires!'

'Find the what?'

'In 1502 a fleet of Spanish treasure ships set off from San Domingo, heading for Spain,' I said dramatically. 'A freak storm sprang up, and they all went down. Only ten wrecks were ever found. Twenty-seven ships, all laden with

Spanish gold, are still somewhere at the bottom of the sea.'

'Hmm!' said Dad.

A few minutes later he looked at his watch, drained his beer in a couple of swallows and tossed money on the table. 'We'd better be getting back to the *Betsey*. Captain Clancy will be ready to sail by now.'

I swigged down my Coke and followed him out.

'That waiter was taking a great interest in our conversation,' said Dad as we walked away.

I looked over my shoulder. Sure enough, the cut-throat waiter was standing in his doorway, staring after us.

I grinned. 'So much the better for our cover story. The more he spreads the word, the better we'll be established as genuine treasure hunters!'

Clancy and Chuck were waiting impatiently when we got back to the *Betsey*.

'Where'd you guys get to?' demanded Chuck.

'We've been establishing our cover story,' I said, and told him about the waterside café.

'You had a drink in Rico's?' asked Clancy incredulously.

'Why shouldn't we?' asked Dad.

Clancy shook his head. 'It's not a place for tourists. Rico's a Marelito, one of the crooks Castro let out of jail just so they could come to America. Every cut-throat and smuggler on the waterfront hangs out in that place.'

Pretty soon the *Betsey* weighed anchor, cast off and did all the other nautical-type things boats do at the beginning of voyages – don't ask me, I'm no sailor – and we set off.

The sea was calm, the sky was blue and the sun beat down. For the first part of the trip we were accompanied by a string of smaller boats, all carrying keen tourist fishermen out to sea. They waved cheerily, and I waved back.

As the journey went on the other ships dropped away behind us. For a while a scruffy-looking fishing boat stayed on our tail, but eventually that too disappeared and we were alone on the limitless blue ocean.

For most of the day I dozed on a mattress on the after-deck. Captain Clancy seemed to have stepped up the speed now we were alone and we were moving along at a surprisingly good clip, leaving a long wake behind. I watched it until I fell asleep...

It was dark when I woke up and the boat had stopped moving.

I was surrounded by darkness.

I jumped up in sudden panic and went into the lighted wheelhouse, where Clancy was showing Dad and Chuck our position on a chart.

'We're pretty close to the area you want by now. I could go on for a while, but we can't do much searching in the dark. I reckon it's best to moor here for the night in the lee of the island. We'll set off at first light.'

So that's what we did.

There was only one guest cabin and of course Dad nabbed that. Clancy and the crew had their own quarters somewhere below, and Chuck and I drew the bunks in the main cabin.

Somehow I couldn't get off to sleep, partly

because I'd slept so much already, partly because of a vague feeling of unease.

I lay there wide awake for a while, listening to Dad's deep rattling snores coming from the nearby cabin, and the lighter ones of Chuck from the bunk opposite. I stood it as long as I could then sat up, put on my trainers – I hadn't bothered to undress – and went on deck.

I stood there straining my eyes in the darkness. The moon was hidden by dark clouds and everything was silent except for the slapping of the waves against the hull. Over to the left I could just make out the darker shape of the island Chuck had mentioned.

I looked at the distant sea and saw a light moving towards me.

A tiny point of light at first, it turned into a glowing sphere as it rushed silently down out of the sky, getting closer and closer.

It descended into the sea somewhere just ahead of us...

Minutes later it reappeared, rising out of the waves and heading back the way it had come.

Chapter Three

USO

I ran into the wheelhouse where Clancy was on watch.

'Did you see that?'

'See what?'

'Some kind of glowing sphere in the sky.'

Clancy gave me a resigned look. 'Probably just another shooting star. Don't worry about it, son.'

'Shooting star nothing,' I said indignantly. 'It came out of the sea somewhere way ahead of us, and then landed quite close. A few minutes later it took off again and flew back the way it came. I'm sure it's something to do with what we're looking for.'

'If you say so,' said Clancy, clearly not believing it for a moment. 'Where did this here USO come down?'

'This here what?'

'USO. Unidentified Submerged Object.'

I pointed out to sea. 'It went into the sea just – there! Then it came out again, from the same place.'

Clancy sighted along my arm and drew a largish circle in pencil on his chart. ' "Just there" is hard to judge at sea and at night, but it should be somewhere in the area I've marked. I guess we could always check it out when it gets light.'

I went back to my bunk convinced I'd be too excited to sleep. I lay there for a while trying to work out the meaning of what I'd seen. Why had the glowing sphere come out of the sea and then gone back underwater? Did it have anything to do with our being in the area?

I was still puzzling over the mystery when I fell asleep.

The smell of coffee woke me up, and I sat up, had a quick wash and joined the others for an early breakfast.

I told them all about my USO sighting, but nobody was very impressed.

Chuck's reaction was exactly the same as Clancy's.

'Probably just a shooting star.'

'It was definitely not a shooting star,' I yelled. 'It came out of the sea, somewhere way in the distance, and went back into the sea somewhere pretty close to us. After a bit it came back up again, and went back the way it had come. It was a kind of fuzzy, glowing sphere.'

'All right, Matthew,' said Dad soothingly. 'Remember, it was late and you were tired. You're quite sure it wasn't a shooting star or a meteor shower, or something like that?'

'It wasn't all that late and I wasn't tired,' I said. 'I'd been sleeping for most of the afternoon. And it didn't feel like a shooting star. It was being guided. It had a direction, a purpose...'

'Listen, kid, we've got an important job to do here,' said Chuck. 'We can't afford to waste time chasing after lights in the sky.'

He looked at Dad. 'I say we ignore young Matthew's meteor.'

If there's one thing Dad hates it's people taking his decisions for him, brushing his opinions aside. Since he sees me as a sort of extension of himself, he doesn't like people doing it to me either.

'And exactly how do you suggest we go about doing this important job, Mr Roberts?' he said smoothly.

'Well, I guess we ought to just – search,' said Chuck defensively. 'Search the whole area.'

'I see,' said Dad. 'Three of us in one small ship, searching an area that has already been searched, as Captain Clancy informed us, by an entire fleet of ships and planes?'

Chuck didn't reply.

'I'm a rational man myself,' said Dad. 'Unfortunately, it seems that all rational means have already been tried and they have failed. We are now reduced to trying the irrational, the unexplained. And if that means chasing Matthew's lights in the sky, that's exactly what we'll do! Is that clear, Mr Roberts? Or shall we cable your Mr Simmonds and determine exactly who is in charge of this expedition?'

At this rather tricky point, Captain Clancy came into the saloon. 'What course do I steer?' he asked – and looked round, sensing the atmosphere.

'I understand my son told you about seeing

a glowing sphere in the sky last night?'

'It was probably just – '

Dad cut him off. 'Yes, I know, just a shooting star. All the same I'd be obliged if you'd set a course for the point where my son saw it enter and leave the water.'

Clancy looked doubtfully at Chuck.

'Do as the professor asks, please, Captain,' said Chuck at last.

'Right away, if you please, Captain Clancy,' said Dad.

Clancy gave him a mocking salute. 'Aye, aye, sir!'

He left the saloon, and a few minutes later we felt the ship changing course.

After a moment Chuck said, 'Sorry if I got out of line, sir. This is my first major assignment for the Agency, and I guess I'm being over-enthusiastic.'

'Forget it,' said Dad, prepared to be generous in victory. 'It's a worrying and frustrating business for us all. But since we don't really know what we're doing, I suppose it doesn't much matter what we do!'

We were just finishing our second cups of

coffee when Captain Clancy came into the saloon.

'Something kinda odd's turned up,' he announced.

Dad looked up. 'What?'

Clancy gave me a rather embarrassed look. 'There seems to be something weird happening on the sea bed – just about where the kid says he saw the USO come down.'

'What sort of a something?' snapped Dad.

'Come and take a look.'

We all crowded into the wheelhouse and studied the screen on the *Betsey*'s ultra-modern control console. As Chuck had told us, the old tub was fitted out with all the latest hi-tech equipment. This included a device for scanning the bottom of the sea bed.

There wasn't a lot to see on the screen, just a lot of murk with something pulsing steadily at the centre.

'What is it?' demanded Dad.

'According to my charts it's the wreck of an old Japanese freighter, the *Kobaru*. Disappeared way back in the thirties, and wasn't found until fifty years later.'

'Danger like dagger,' I said.

Everyone stared at me.

'Sorry,' I said. 'Just something I read in a book about the Bermuda Triangle. It was part of the last message from a missing Japanese ship. The pilot of our missing plane said something about a dagger as well.'

'What's so odd about finding an old wreck?' asked Dad. 'Especially since you already knew it was there!'

Chuck shook his head. 'The thing is, it's giving off some kind of low-level radiation, seems to be confusing the instruments.'

'Any idea what might be causing it?' I asked.

Chuck shrugged. 'Could be anything! No way to tell from up here.'

I looked at Dad. 'Is the radiation harmful?'

Dad checked Clancy's instrument panel. 'It shouldn't be, not for a relatively brief exposure.'

'How deep is the wreck?' I asked Clancy.

'Somewhere around a hundred feet.'

'We'll have to go down and take a look,' I said. 'Have you got any diving equipment?'

We anchored close to the USO site and got ready to make the dive.

It turned out that Clancy only had two diving outfits and there was quite a bit of wrangling about who was going to wear them.

'There's no question of your going, Matthew,' said Dad. 'I just won't hear of it. I shall go myself!'

'There's a lot more sense in my going than you going,' I said. 'Have you ever scuba-dived in your life?'

'Have you?'

'Three holidays in the Med,' I said triumphantly. 'And I've been to scuba-diving school and got a Certificate of Competence. Let's face it, Dad, if you insist on going you'll just be a liability to whoever dives with you.' I pressed home my advantage. 'I'm an experienced scuba-diver and what's more, I'm your resident alien expert. I'm the logical choice to be one of the divers.'

You can always get Dad by appealing to logic.

'And I'm the other one,' said Chuck. 'Scuba-diving's been a hobby of mine for years, I know these waters, and I'm the official representative of the Agency!'

Dad didn't like it, but in the end he was forced to give way.

With the arguing over, Chuck, who was the real expert, laid the gear out on the deck and checked it over carefully.

'Diving suits, masks, hoods, gloves, fins, weight belts, two air-tanks each, two diver's knives with sheaths and leg-straps, one Halogen lamp...'

'You're very cautious,' said Dad approvingly.

'Pays to be,' said Chuck seriously. 'It's carelessness gets you killed. Don't worry, Professor, I've done over a hundred dives. I'll take good care of your boy.'

We climbed into the gear, and when everything was in place and checked over once again, we sat up on the rail, backs to the sea.

'You won't be able to stay down too long,' warned Clancy. 'Just take a look and come back up again.'

Dad said, 'Take care, Matthew.'

Chuck put on his mask and looped the cord

of the Halogen lamp around his wrist. He put in his mouth-piece, and checked his airflow.

'Ready, Matt?'

'Ready,' I said.

Chuck went backwards over the rail and disappeared beneath the surface.

A few seconds later, I followed him.

I went down under *Betsey*'s keel and then followed the anchor line downwards. The water was quite warm and amazingly clear and I could see Chuck swimming downwards ahead of me. We followed the anchor line down to the bottom and there, about a hundred yards away, was the dark bulk of the wreck.

It was sitting, still upright, in a little gully on the sea bed.

It was some kind of freighter or cargo-vessel, and it looked as if it had been there for a very long time. The rusting hull was overgrown with weeds.

There was light coming from somewhere inside the ship. Its eerie glow silhouetted the freighter's deck-rails.

I swam up beside Chuck and he pointed towards the glow.

I nodded and we swam towards the freighter.

We reached the freighter and let ourselves sink gently down on to the deck, holding on to the rails.

The light was coming from a partly-opened hatchway. I swam towards it and tugged it open. Chuck swam up beside me, tapped me on the shoulder and shook his head.

Ignoring him, I plunged through the open hatchway.

I was in some kind of cabin, perhaps the main saloon.

A skeleton lay stretched out on the main bunk. I had an irrational fear that it was going to sit up, but it didn't move.

The light-source was coming from somewhere further ahead and I swam towards it, Chuck close behind me.

The saloon led into a metal corridor and at the end of the corridor was a steep stairway leading downwards. We swam down it and found ourselves in the main hold.

The light-source was there at the far end.

It consisted of a pulsing, glowing pod

attached to the steel wall of the hold. It was semi-transparent and packed with a web of complex coils. The whole thing seemed to be not so much manufactured as grown.

Linked to the pod by a network of cables were four transparent capsules, rather like giant test-tubes.

Three were empty. The fourth held the body of a man.

We swam up closer. The man was black-haired and thin and he was wearing some kind of uniform. His face was marble-white and it was impossible to tell whether he was alive or dead.

I looked at Chuck, wondering what we should do next.

We could hardly leave the man there.

On the other hand, if he was alive, we might kill him by trying to move him.

Chuck however wasn't suffering from any doubts. He drew the diver's knife strapped to his leg and began slashing at the cables attaching the fourth tube to the pod.

It was quite a job. There were a lot of cables and they seemed to be tough and sinewy.

Chuck hacked away at them determinedly. Since we were committed now, I drew my own diver's knife and started helping him.

At last the pod came free and began floating away from the wall. Chuck grabbed it and started steering it towards the stairway. I moved closer and did my best to help him.

We manoeuvred the capsule across the hold and up the steps. Behind us the main pod was pulsing angrily. I had a nasty feeling that we'd triggered some kind of self-destruct mechanism.

We steered the capsule up the steps, along the corridor, through the saloon with its sleeping skeleton and up onto the deck.

All the time the light from the pod was flashing more brightly and more rapidly. There was no sound, but you could feel the energy pulsing through the water.

Chuck jettisoned some of his belt-weights, I did the same, and we floated rapidly upwards, holding the capsule between us.

When we broke the surface we saw the

anxious heads of Dad, Clancy and the crew lining *Betsey*'s rail.

I climbed rapidly up the ladder, leaving Chuck supporting the capsule, and tore off my face mask.

'Get Chuck and that capsule thing out of the water right away,' I ordered.

'The minute you've done that, Captain Clancy, get us out of here just as quick as you can. We triggered off something in that wreck and I think it's about to blow.'

Such was the urgency in my voice that nobody argued. Clancy and his crew rigged up some kind of cat's-cradle of ropes and hauled the capsule out of the water with amazing speed.

Chuck climbed the ladder, and the minute his finned feet touched the deck the *Betsey* was on the move.

Even so, we were only just in time.

The water over the wreck was already starting to boil.

Soon the boiling became a whirlpool, and that turned into a giant water-spout.

There was the dull thud of an undersea

explosion and bits of the shattered *Kobaru* started raining down out of the sky.

Luckily most of it missed us, although a chunk of rusty steel plate made a nasty dent in the wheelhouse roof.

Dad and Chuck got the white-faced man out of the capsule, down into the saloon and laid him on the bunk.

Dad made a rapid examination, and I remembered thankfully that he numbered a medical qualification amongst his numerous degrees.

'Well, he's still alive,' he said calmly. 'I think he's been in suspended animation, possibly under some kind of cryogenic process, but it doesn't seem to have done him much harm. If we keep him warm he should make a full recovery.'

He spread all our blankets over the still form. Already normal colour was beginning to come back into the white face.

'We were dead lucky,' I told Chuck reproachfully. 'Or rather, he was! Didn't it occur to you that we might finish him off just by trying to move him?'

'Of course it did,' said Chuck impatiently. 'But considering who he is I had to take the chance.'

'What do you mean, considering who he is?' asked Dad.

'Didn't I show you the dossiers? No, maybe I didn't...'

Chuck reached for the briefcase he'd brought on board with him. He opened the complicated top-security lock and took out three black plastic folders. Each one had 'TOP SECRET' stamped across the front.

Chuck opened the folders, one by one and displayed them on the table. Each folder contained a glossy head-and-shoulders portrait with a typed label stuck on underneath.

The first folder showed a tough looking middle-aged lady with iron-grey hair. She looked like the headmistress of a very exclusive school.

'Mrs Linda Billington,' said Chuck. 'Boss lady of British security. They call her the Maggie Thatcher of the Intelligence world.'

He opened the second folder and showed us the picture of a handsome middle-aged man with a long, thin, aristocratic face.

'Monsieur Paul D'Arigny, Head of the Combined French Intelligence Committee.'

Chuck opened the third folder, to show a balding middle-aged man with a face like an exceptionally grumpy bulldog.

'And last, but I hope not least, our own beloved General Mike Morrisey, head of the Agency.'

'Fascinating,' said Dad. 'And the man you rescued?'

Chuck fished another dossier out of the briefcase. It was blue, not black, and it had no TOP SECRET stamp. It showed a dark-haired young man in Army uniform.

'Lieutenant Bill Palmer of the United States Army Air Force,' said Chuck. 'He was piloting the missing plane.'

As if roused by the sound of his name the man on the bunk stirred and muttered feebly.

Chuck leaned over him. 'Lieutenant Palmer? Bill! Can you hear me?'

Palmer stared blankly at him and muttered, 'Thirsty...'

Chuck held a mug of water to his lips and he took a few sips.

'Can you tell us what happened?' asked Chuck urgently. 'Do you know where the others are?'

'Everything strange,' said Palmer feebly. 'Sea all wrong, sky all wrong. Lost...couldn't find coast.'

'That's right,' said Chuck. 'You reported back to the control tower. Everything seemed strange and your instruments didn't work. *What happened after that?*'

Palmer just stared at him. He seemed to be sinking back into unconsciousness.

'What about the dagger?' I asked.

'You saw something,' I said. 'Something like a dagger...'

His eyes widened and he stared at me in panic.

Suddenly Palmer began thrashing to and fro on the bunk.

His voice rose to a hoarse scream. 'No, keep it away. It's a giant dagger – a dagger of the sea...'

Chapter Four

HIJACK

It took us quite a while to calm poor Palmer down. Eventually Dad had to give him an injection from the ship's medical kit.

'Sorry about all that,' I said when he sank into unconsciousness at last. 'I hoped that dagger business might trigger something in his memory. All it did was make him hysterical.'

Dad straightened up from his examination of Palmer's still form.

'It might be possible to get something out of him when he recovers – through regressive hypnosis maybe. But we can't do much here. He really ought to be in hospital.'

'Should we turn back?' I asked.

'Not now,' protested Chuck. 'Not just when we seem to be getting somewhere!'

'I'm not prepared to endanger this man's life,' said Dad.

Chuck said, 'More lives than his are at stake here...'

It looked as if a promising row was brewing up.

'Let's ask Captain Clancy,' I suggested. 'Maybe he can come up with something.'

Fortunately he could. 'No need to turn back,' he said. 'I can radio the nearest Naval base and they'll send out a rescue helicopter. They'll get him into hospital a lot quicker than we could.'

So that's what we did. Clancy sent his message and we settled down to wait at anchor just off one of the islands. Eventually we heard the clattering roar of a big Navy helicopter.

We lashed Palmer to a stretcher and took him back on deck. The helicopter hovered over the *Betsey*, lowered a complicated harness and whisked the stretcher, and Palmer, into its interior. A few minutes later the helicopter disappeared in the direction of Miami, and we all settled down in the saloon for a conference.

Naturally, Dad took command. 'Well, now,'

he began. 'What do we make of all this? Matthew, you're our self-styled alien expert.'

'Just a minute now,' objected Chuck. 'Are we simply going to assume extra-terrestrial involvement?'

'As a working hypothesis, yes,' said Dad. 'I'm as sceptical as the next man, but in the circumstances, I really don't see what else we can do.'

'You know what we saw down in that ship, Chuck,' I said. 'Don't you think it was just a touch beyond Fidel Castro, the Russians, or any other of the traditional enemies of the American way of life?'

'I guess so,' said Chuck reluctantly.

'Go on, Matthew,' said Dad. 'What do you make of what's happened?'

'Well, as a working hypothesis, let's take it that the aliens abducted our three VIPs. There were four capsules in that hold, remember, and three of them were empty. I think they hid the VIPs and their pilot in that old sunken ship, close to the actual abduction site.'

'Why the heck would they bother to do that?' asked Chuck.

'Perhaps they were waiting until the search died down. One thing we do know about them is that they hate to be seen.

'Anyway, when things quieten down they send some kind of craft to the freighter to pick up the three VIPs.'

'A craft which you just happen to see,' said Chuck.

'That might have just been simple coincidence,' I said. 'They had to come some time and we *were* in the area.' A sudden thought came into my mind. 'Or – maybe they wanted to be seen.'

'Why?' asked Dad.

'Who knows? Why did they leave the pilot behind?'

'Perhaps they didn't have any use for him,' said Chuck.

'Maybe not,' I said. 'Or maybe they wanted him found – to let us know they have the other three. When we found the pilot and the three empty capsules, that was a pretty obvious conclusion. And since they'd gone to some trouble to keep the pilot alive, it seems logical to assume that the others are alive as well.

Maybe they wanted us to know that too.'

'Which leads us to the next question,' said Dad. 'Why kidnap them at all?'

'Which, in turn, brings us to Operation Thunderball,' I said.

'To what?' snapped Dad.

'Don't you remember?' I said. 'Chuck mentioned it at that first meeting back in Miami.'

'I'm not allowed to talk about Operation Thunderball,' said Chuck obstinately. 'It's classified, strictly need-to-know.'

'For heaven's sake stop this ridiculous cloak-and-dagger, James Bond mumbo-jumbo,' roared Dad. '*We* need to know, if we're going to help you.'

Chuck shook his head, closed his mouth and tightened his lips.

'It's all right, Chuck,' I said soothingly. 'You can't talk about it, but I can. You referred to Operation Thunderball in Simmonds' office and he jumped right in and shut you up. Why was he so concerned? I've been thinking about it, on and off, ever since.'

Chuck still kept silent.

'Tell us what you've been thinking, Matthew,' urged Dad.

I looked hard at Chuck. 'I think Dad's crack about James Bond was bang on,' I said.

' "Thunderball" was the name of one of the old Bond movies. Something about stealing atomic missiles, I think. It's a nice dramatic sort of word. Just the sort of word to appeal to some gung-ho character as code name for an aggressive operation involving atomic missiles. Am I right, Chuck?'

Chuck said, 'How did you – ' and clamped his mouth shut again.

'Suppose some high-powered military types decided that aliens were operating from undersea bases here in the Triangle,' I said. 'Suppose those same military types decided to winkle out the aliens with a few well-placed atomic depth-charges?'

It was quite clear from the expression on Chuck's face that my guess had been accurate.

'Tut tut,' said Dad reprovingly. 'That's very bad security.'

'What is?' asked Chuck faintly.

'Using a name like Thunderball.'

Chuck looked at me unbelievingly. 'How could you possibly guess so much so accurately – just from hearing the name?'

Dad launched into another of his lectures.

'During the war, Winston Churchill ordered that the code names for all military operations should be totally meaningless. If the name had a meaning, someone on the other side might be able to work out what that meaning was, you see – exactly as Matthew did just now. Arnhem was called Market Garden, as I remember, and the Normandy invasion was Overlord...'

'All right, Dad, I think you've made your point.' I turned to Chuck. 'I think this whole abduction business is a reaction to Operation Thunderball. It didn't destroy the aliens, it just made them angry. So they kidnapped your VIPs by way of retaliation. I don't know if they knew they were VIPs or if it was just pure chance. But I do know that the first thing to do is to call off Operation Thunderball, before it does any more harm.'

'I can send a coded cable to Simmonds

explaining your theories,' said Chuck. 'Though whether it'll do any good... What do we do now?'

'We just go on heading into the Triangle,' I said. 'The aliens have already made contact after a fashion. Maybe they'll do it again. Or maybe they won't. All we can do is be ready.'

Chuck went off to send his cable. After a while he came back looking worried.

'I've sent a long cable to Simmonds outlining your ideas and recommending in the strongest terms that Thunderball be discontinued,' he said. 'Now there's another complication.'

'What's that?' I asked.

'Clancy's picked up a distress signal from some cabin cruiser.' He sighed. 'Apparently we're nearest, so we have to turn back and help them. Sacred rule of the sea and all that. I tried to talk Clancy out of it but he threatened to throw me overboard.'

'Quite right too,' I said. 'Never mind, Chuck, it'll make a nice change from our other problems.'

'Sure,' said Chuck gloomily. 'Like hitting

your thumb with a hammer, instead of banging your head against the wall!'

We felt the ship change course.

One of the crew served a snack lunch of sandwiches and coffee and by the time it was over the distressed vessel was in sight.

It was a scruffy looking fishing vessel, bobbing up and down in the sea swell, apparently deserted.

We all went up on deck to have a look.

'What exactly was the emergency?' asked Dad.

'Message was pretty vague,' said Clancy.

'Maybe the engine's broken down and they're all down below trying to fix it,' said Chuck.

'Who knows?' said Clancy. 'Dumb fishermen. That tub doesn't look seaworthy anyway.' He called the crew.

'Take the dinghy and get over there. Take a first aid kit in case someone's hurt. Take a tool kit too, see if you can get them moving again. Otherwise we may have to give them a tow.'

We watched as a couple of the crew put a

tool kit and a first aid box into the dinghy, lowered it over the side, climbed in and rowed over to the stranded ship.

We watched them tie up to the fishing vessel and go below.

For quite a long time nothing happened. Then the crewmen came back up on deck, followed by two others, small dark men in seamen's overalls. All four climbed into the dinghy and the crewmen rowed it back towards us.

'What the blazes are they bringing 'em back here for?' grumbled Clancy.

The boat rowed across to us and tied up to the boarding ladder. One of the strangers climbed quickly up the ladder and suddenly produced a sub-machine gun from beneath his overalls.

'Back,' he ordered. 'Back away from the ladder.'

We obeyed and Clancy's two crewmen climbed the ladder, another armed man behind them.

'Sorry, Captain,' said one of the crewmen. 'We went down below and they were waiting for us with Uzis.'

Captain Clancy was outraged. 'This is piracy!'

'Yeah, sure,' said the first man in a bored tone. He turned to his accomplice. 'Take the boat back across and fetch the boss.'

The second man jumped back in the boat and rowed back towards the cabin cruiser. The rest of us waited on deck under the menace of the gun.

'Nobody try anything,' warned the gunman. He patted the gun. 'Or I cut you all down, no trouble at all.'

I wondered if Chuck was still wearing his gun – and then remembered seeing him put it away in the saloon locker just after we cast off. It was probably just as well. Resistance could get us all killed.

The dinghy returned and its passenger climbed up the ladder and looked arrogantly around the deck. He had a drooping moustache, an unshaven chin and burning black eyes.

He also had a machine gun.

He looked strangely familiar and suddenly I

realised – he was the waiter who'd served us at Rico's, the waterfront café where we'd had a drink before setting off.

He saw he'd been recognised and grinned triumphantly.

'Pretty clever hey? I hear you talking at my bar, hear you talk about treasure, hear you mention Clancy's name. Everyone know Captain Clancy and his ship *Betsey*. Big time treasure hunter. I tell my smuggler friends and we follow you. We send Mayday call, set up ambush!' He gestured to Clancy and his crew with his machine gun. 'Carlos! Take them below, lock them up.' He pointed at Chuck. 'Him too!'

When the others were locked up and his man came back on deck Rico turned to us. 'Now we talk!'

'What do you want?' demanded Dad.

'All very simple,' said Rico cheerfully. 'You tell us where treasure is, we give you a fair share. Otherwise we kill you.'

'There isn't any treasure, you fool,' said Dad angrily. 'Or if there is, we know nothing about it.'

'Oh sure,' jeered Rico. 'You don't know nothing about Spanish galleons filled with gold under the sea. That's why you come all the way from England, hire Captain Clancy's boat, and set off into Devil's Triangle.'

Rico brandished his sub-machine gun. 'Well? You gonna tell me? Or do I start killing you, one by one?' He jabbed the gun at me. 'Start with you.' He swung the gun round on Dad. 'Or maybe kill old man first, no use anyway.'

'You don't want to bother with him,' I said. 'I know where the treasure is.'

'Okay,' said Rico. 'You tell me.'

'I'll do a deal with you,' I said.

'Matthew!' said Dad.

'Ignore him,' I said quickly. 'He's greedy, he doesn't want to share. Me, I'd sooner share than get shot.'

'Sensible,' said Rico. 'So, you tell me where treasure is?'

I shook my head. 'I won't tell you, but I'll take you there. We can go in your ship and leave all this lot behind. No share for them, just you and me.'

Rico considered for a minute or two, while I held my breath. Would he go for it? It was a slender chance, but it was the only one we had.

At last he said, 'All right, it's a deal.' He turned to one of his gang. 'Smash their radio so they can't send messages. Then we go.'

One of the gang went into the wheelhouse and we heard the sound of smashing machinery.

'Matt, don't do this,' said Dad. He turned to Rico. 'Don't listen to him, there isn't any treasure. We came out here hunting for aliens...'

'Sure you did,' said Rico. 'You're not after gold, you chase little green men!'

I'd done too good a job with my sunken treasure ship cover story. Now Rico wouldn't believe the truth when he heard it.

I looked hard at Dad and said, 'Maybe we'll meet some little green men after all. There's always a chance.'

'Okay we go,' said Rico when his man came back from the wheelhouse. 'Anyone tries to stop us, we shoot you all. If you try to attack us at sea we kill the boy straight away.'

I went on looking at Dad. 'He means it,' I said. 'Don't get us killed for nothing. This way there's a chance.'

'Good luck, Matthew,' said Dad quietly.

I went down the ladder and jumped into the dinghy. Minutes later I was climbing on board Rico's boat. Very soon the engine coughed into life and we roared away at a surprising speed. Like the *Betsey* Rico's ship was a lot faster than she looked.

'Good boat this,' boasted Rico as we roared ahead. 'Smugglers' boat, very fast. Once we're sure treasure is there we come back with bigger boat, proper diving gear and everything we need. Now you take us to treasure! How you hear about it anyway?'

I spun him a complicated yarn about finding a treasure map in an old book in the British Museum. I told him we'd left the map at home and memorised the coordinates for the place where the treasure lay. Rico lapped it all up, dreaming of future riches.

The day wore on and we sped deeper and deeper into the heart of the Bermuda Triangle.

We were heading for the spot where I'd seen the glowing sphere make its final descent into the sea. I stood on the fore-deck just in front of the cabin. I was thinking hard, but my thoughts were far away.

I was thinking of the red desert in the heart of Australia, of Corroboree rock and a limp alien form on a stretcher.

I was seeing a great glowing sphere suddenly appearing from nowhere in the desert.

During my researches into the paranormal I'd read that telepathy, if it existed at all, might well be able to transcend space and time.

I was hoping desperately that what I'd read was true.

Suddenly the sea ahead of me began to look strange. The sky was strange too and the air seemed suddenly opaque. Even the roar of the engine sounded different.

Rico and the others noticed too. They stopped their endless chattering and looked uneasily at each other.

Rico came up to me and grabbed my arm. 'Something wrong!'

I ignored him and stared straight ahead.

Suddenly the sea became solid and rose up before us.

A tall glowing column appeared, thick at the top, pointed at the bottom – like a giant dagger.

I seemed to see dim shapes moving inside it.

Reacting in the only way they knew how, Rico and his men raised their guns.

'No!' I shouted. 'Whatever you do, don't attack it.'

Rico raised his gun and fired a long burst at the column.

One by one his men all opened fire.

A needle-point ray of light sprang out of the column and touched Rico briefly. He screamed, his body glowed and he collapsed, a charred and smoking corpse.

One by one his men suffered the same terrible fate.

Soon I was the only one left alive on the little fishing boat.

I spread out my hands to show that I was unarmed and waited.

Another, thicker beam of light sprang out

from the fiery column and touched the fishing boat's hull.

As the ship exploded I was hurled through the air – into the heart of the glowing, dagger-shaped alien column as it sank beneath the sea.

Chapter Five

TRIBUNAL

I awoke in a glowing white chamber, lying on a ledge set into the wall. The chamber walls were made of some semi-transparent substance, lit by its own inner glow. The substance was something like crystal, something like porcelain, yet somehow warmer, more malleable, more alive than either.

I sat up and looked across the chamber. On the other side were three transparent capsules. One held a grey-haired stern featured woman, the second a slender aristocratic-looking man, the third a thick-set man with a face like a grumpy bulldog.

I had found my three missing VIPs. The problem now was to get them out of here – wherever here was – alive. And myself too, of course.

I looked around the chamber, but there

didn't seem to be any door. I stood up and the ledge faded into the wall. I sat down and suddenly the ledge reappeared.

I realised that I was thirsty – and hungry as well. As the thought formed itself in my mind a cavity appeared in the wall beside me. It held a goblet full of some clear liquid and a platter with a few scraps of food. Goblet and platter were in the same milky substance as the chamber itself.

I lifted the goblet and sipped cautiously at the liquid. It was water, clear and cold and so pure that it must have been distilled.

I swigged down the lot.

The food was rather more of a problem. It was cold and clammy and fishy and rubbery. I told myself it was no worse than sushi and made myself swallow a few of the smaller bits, just to be polite. It looked as if my unseen hosts weren't big eaters anyway. I put the goblet and platter back into the alcove and it closed up again.

At least I seemed to be communicating with the chamber. Maybe I could communicate with its owners as well. Maybe they were all part of the same thing.

I sat on the ledge and waited, studying the featureless room.

I had the strangest feeling that the room was studying me.

I tried to keep my mind calm and peaceful. I suppose I must have been scared – but feelings of excitement and curiosity were just as strong.

Suddenly I felt a kind of mental summons. I stood up and a glowing tunnel opened before me. I walked along it and entered a larger chamber. A ledge ran around the edge to form a seat and a mushroom-shaped table rose in the centre.

I looked around the chamber and there they were – a dozen slender silver-clad forms with greeny-grey skin and slanting green eyes in long narrow faces.

We stood looking at each other in mutual astonishment. I suddenly realised that they were as wary of me as I was of them.

I realised too that I was one of comparatively few humans that they had even attempted to communicate with. Humans like me, anyway. They seemed to have developed some kind of relationship with the Australian aborigines, the Angaru. But the Angaru were special. So-called civilised people – like me – were a mystery to them.

We sat for a long time in that strange, glowing chamber exchanging – what? Not words, certainly, but thoughts, feelings, emotions. I tried to give them a sort of potted history of humanity, evolving from a savage ape, fighting amongst ourselves, but gradually, agonisingly slowly, evolving, improving.

I tried to tell them that although many on our planet would greet them with fear and hostility, many, like the Angaru, like me, would like to meet them as friends.

I told them that we needed time.

I don't know how much got through. I sensed that they must have evolved from some cooler, more passionless species on their distant world and human emotions baffled and frightened them.

Finally the attempts at communication, such as they were, were over, and the aliens went into conference amongst themselves. I could dimly sense that there were differing opinions. Some, I think, had already decided that we were dangerous beasts who should be destroyed. Others were prepared to reserve judgement.

Finally one of them, their leader perhaps – if they had leaders – led me back down the tunnel to the original, smaller chamber. The three occupied capsules still stood against the wall, but now there was a fourth, an empty one with its front standing open.

It was pretty obvious what I was supposed to do next. I realised that I didn't really know what had been the verdict of this strange alien tribunal.

Had I been found guilty or not guilty?

Had I been pardoned or condemned?

I stood there for a moment, uncertain whether the capsule meant freedom, a death sentence, or just a permanent place in some alien museum.

The alien stretched out a slender, four fingered hand. I held my hand out and just for a moment, our fingers touched.

Feeling somehow reassured, I stepped inside the capsule and it closed around me.

It was calm and quiet and incredibly soothing and I slipped almost at once into unconsciousness...

When I awoke I was lying on a bunk on board *Betsey* with Dad looking down at me. I was both touched and embarrassed to see that there were tears in his eyes.

Some time later, when I was wide awake and drinking strong sweet tea, Dad told me what had been happening.

After I'd gone off with Rico and his merry band they'd waited on the *Betsey* in agonised indecision, wondering what to do next.

Finally they'd decided on an attempt at rescue. They were pretty sure Rico was going to shoot me anyway as soon as he discovered the treasure didn't exist. So they might as well try to save me first.

If they failed – well, at least there was vengeance.

Clancy had opened the weapons locker and armed to the teeth they'd chugged cautiously after us, planning to follow at extreme range and attack under cover of darkness.

Meanwhile they'd taken it in turns to observe Rico's ship by telescope. It was Dad who'd seen it explode in a cloud of smoke and flame. Naturally he'd thought everything was over.

By now it was getting dark, and they'd decided to stay in the area overnight and search for wreckage – and bodies – in the morning. They had no hopes at all that I'd survived.

I shuddered at the memory of my narrow escape.

'So what happened next?'

'You just – popped up!' said Dad.

'We were just about to start the search when something bobbed up beside the boat. It was you, in one of those capsule things. Then three more popped up and there were our three potted VIPs. So we hauled you back on board and that was that.'

Mrs Billington was occupying the guest cabin while General Morrisey and D'Arigny were on the two bunks – I could see their blanket-wrapped forms. Apparently they'd been harder to arouse than I had, but Dad was pretty sure that they'd all be able to appear at the vital Intelligence Conference. Now we were heading back for Miami at top speed.

'Well, that's our side of it,' said Dad. 'So what happened to you?'

Chuck and Clancy leaned forward eagerly.

'Yeah, come on,' said Chuck. 'Tell us what happened!'

I drew a deep breath. 'Well...'

I did my best to tell them but it wasn't easy to put over, and I'm not sure how much they understood or even believed. Finally Dad said I was getting over tired and insisted that I be allowed to rest...

I got another chance a few days later when Dad and I were summoned to a final meeting with Mr Simmonds in his Miami conference room.

Also present were Chuck Roberts, Mrs Billington, Monsieur D'Arigny and General Morrisey.

The last three had no clear memory of events between things going wrong with their flight and waking up on board *Betsey*. They had to accept that they'd been abducted by aliens but they certainly didn't want to dwell on it.

The purpose of the meeting was to make top level recommendations for an Alien Encounter Policy.

As resident alien expert, to use Dad's phrase, I was listened to with flattering attention.

'Given that these – alien beings – exist, young fellow,' boomed General Morrisey, 'what are we to do about them?'

'Nothing,' I said.

Mrs Billington frowned. 'Nothing?'

'But surely,' began D'Arigny.

'Nothing!' I said firmly. 'Nothing at all. Don't chase them, don't poke them and certainly don't shoot atomic missiles at them.'

'Don't worry,' said General Morrisey. 'Operation Thunderball has been permanently closed down.'

'Good! The thing to remember about the aliens,' I went on, 'is that they're shy. They don't want any Close Encounters. That's why they chose the loneliest places on Earth to land, the heart of the desert or the depths of the ocean. I think they find us rather alarming. There are too many of us and we move too fast. In 1845 the desert was empty, by 1945 there was a radar tracking station. Suddenly the oceans are crowded with ships and the skies with planes. They must feel that they keep tripping over us!'

'These strange events in the Bermuda Triangle,' said Mrs Billington. 'Surely they are evidence of hostile activity?'

'I don't think so,' I said. 'The arrival and departure of their craft, the energy emissions from their bases have often caused problems, but I don't think it was deliberate.'

'If they don't want anything to do with us, why do they come here?' demanded D'Arigny indignantly.

'I've no idea,' I said helplessly. 'I don't think you need fear anything like conquest; they're simply not interested. If we leave them alone and don't fuss them – maybe we'll find out!'

'Do you think they'll take your advice?' asked Dad, as we settled down next day for the long flight home.

'About leaving the aliens alone? I doubt it. Human beings are like Kipling's Elephant's Child. We suffer from insatiable curiosity!'

Dad nodded. 'It's a bit of an affront to human dignity as well.'

'What is?'

'Realising that although we're fascinated by them, they couldn't care less about us!'

I nodded. To be honest I was as guilty as anyone else of curiosity about the aliens.

What did they want on Earth?

What did they really think of us?

Could we ever be friends?

'One day, perhaps,' I thought. 'One day...'

I remembered the touch of alien fingers on my own.

Perhaps, in a small way, I had made a start...